J series

BIONICLE™

CHRONICLES #4

The Tales of the Masks

by Greg Farshtey

SCHOLASTIC INC.
New York   Toronto   London   Auckland   Sydney
Mexico City   New Delhi   Hong Kong   Buenos Aires

ISBN 0-439-60706-X

12   6 7 8/0

Printed in the U.S.A.
First printing, December 2003

The Legend of Mata Nui

In the time before time, the Great Spirit descended from the heavens, carrying us, the ones called the Matoran, to this island paradise. We were separate and without purpose, so the Great Spirit blessed us with three virtues: unity, duty, and destiny. We embraced these gifts and, in gratitude, we named our island home Mata Nui, after the Great Spirit himself.

But our happiness was not to last. Mata Nui's brother, Makuta, was jealous of these honors and betrayed him. Makuta cast a spell over Mata Nui, who fell into a deep slumber. Makuta's power dominated the land, as fields withered away, sunlight grew cold, and ancient values were forgotten.

Still, all hope was not lost. Legends told of six mighty heroes, the Toa, who would arrive to save Mata Nui. Time would reveal that these were not simply myths — for the Toa did appear on the shores of the island. They arrived with no memory, no knowledge of one another — but they pledged to defend Mata Nui and its people against the darkness. Tahu, Toa of Fire. Onua, Toa of Earth. Gali, Toa of Water. Lewa, Toa of Air. Pohatu, Toa of Stone. And Kopaka, Toa of Ice. Great warriors with great power, drawn from the very elements themselves. Together, they were six heroes with one destiny: to defeat Makuta and save Mata Nui.

This is their story.

INTRODUCTION

Turaga Vakama, elder of the village of Ta-Koro, sat in silence. The council fire had burned down to ashes. The Matoran, tired from their labors, had gone to sleep and the island of Mata Nui was quiet.

It should have been a time of celebration for the Turaga. The shadow of the insectlike Bohrok swarms and Bohrok-Kal had finally been lifted from the land. The Toa had returned from their struggle and joined with the Matoran to repair damage done to the villages. All were enjoying a rare feeling on Mata Nui: peace.

Only the Turaga stood apart from the joyous work. They knew many secrets about the past and the possible future. The time had come to decide if those secrets should be shared.

"We have to tell the Toa the truth," Turaga Nokama of Ga-Koro insisted. "They have earned this through their great deeds. How many times have they saved us all from Makuta's power?"

Onewa, Turaga of Po-Koro, shook his head. "That is true, sister. But they have done so without knowing any more than was necessary about the past. I prefer it stay that way."

Nokama began to reply but was cut off by an angry string of clicks and whistles coming from Turaga Nuju of Ko-Koro. Matoro, Nuju's interpreter, struggled to keep up with the rapid speech. "Um, Turaga Nuju says . . ." Matoro began. "Oh, no, I can't say that about Turaga Onewa!"

Nokama tried not to smile but failed. Even Vakama chuckled, saying, "Our friends from Ko-Koro always go right to the heart of the matter. Still, Onewa has a point. We know all too well what can happen when knowledge is in the wrong hands."

"We also know, brother, the heartpain of not being trusted ourselves," Turaga Matau from

Le-Koro said. "I say the Toa are wise enough and strong enough to know all. They must know all if they are to fulfill their destiny!"

Onewa slammed his stone hammer on the ground. "Destiny? Let them show unity first! Since they became Toa Nuva, they have done nothing but argue with one another. Kopaka squabbles with Tahu, Gali avoids speaking with either of them . . . are these the acts of worthy Toa?"

"There was a time, hammerer, when Toa argued quite often," said Nokama. "I am quite sure you remember. Yet somehow they found the will to do what had to be done."

"That was . . . different," Onewa replied with a shrug. "Perhaps these Toa do not have the same wisdom."

"Wiselearning is hard to come by, if no one will teach," said Matau.

Whenua, ruler of the underground village of Onu-Koro, had said nothing throughout the debate. He had merely sat and listened to the worry and the anger, the hope and the fear. It was not so different from listening to the sounds of the earth, hearing the approach of a quake or the roar of a subterranean river.

Finally, the wise Turaga rose from his seat and looked around at his old friends. "Brothers . . . and sister . . . the Onu-Matoran live in darkness. It is our way. We thrive where the light does not reach, and when we walk on the surface, we must shield our eyes from the sun's glow."

Nuju clicked something in response. Matoro opened his mouth to translate, but Vakama held up a hand. "Be at ease. I believe we all can guess what he is saying . . . and the answer is Whenua will make his point in his own time, as he has always done."

"When I was younger, I believed all answers could be found in the past," continued Whenua. "I still believe the past should be our teacher. Not so very long ago, the Toa came to our shores and brought hope. They defeated every danger that threatened Mata Nui . . . and as Onewa says, they did it all in darkness. But what more could they have accomplished with the light of truth?"

"I must agree," Nokama said quietly.

"Knowledge, my friends . . . knowledge is the key," Whenua said. "Without it, for all their power, the Toa will not see. We must share our secrets."

Now Vakama rose, firestaff in hand, and lifted his head to look at the six stars in the heavens above. "If they knew . . . If they knew what really happened in Metru Nui, how would they feel? Would they welcome knowing they are not truly alone, or be angry at our deception? How are we to know the right thing to do?"

"The same way we always know," said Nokama. "We turn to the legends. The Toa learned much in their quest for the Kanohi Nuva Masks. Stripped of their powers, they still found a way to succeed. Perhaps in the tales of their adventures, we will find the answers we seek."

"I have heard the tales," answered Vakama.

"Heard, yes . . . but have you listened?" said Nokama.

Vakama thought about her words for a very long time. Perhaps Nokama was right. There might have been something in the Toa's most recent deeds that he had missed.

He returned to his place in the circle. "Once again, the Turaga of water proves to be the wisest of us all. Very well, then. Each of us will tell a tale of the Toa's search for the Kanohi Nuva. At the end of our storytelling, we will make our decision. Now, who shall begin?"

Vakama's answer was a burst of clicks and whistles from Nuju. Matoro nodded and reported, "The Turaga says . . . he says you have all created enough hot air to melt the glaciers of Ko-Wahi. He will tell his tale first, and no more will be needed after that."

"Ha! I sometimes think, brother, that too much time in the ice and snow has caused your brain to freeze," Onewa said. "Allow a true storyteller to share a tale!"

Nokama laid a gentle hand on Nuju's arm. "My friend, I have no doubt your story will be the greatest of all and make ours look poor by comparison. So why not save it until later in the evening, when it will be most appreciated?"

In all the time he had known her, Nuju had never been able to say no to Nokama . . . not for long, anyway. He looked at Vakama and gave a nod.

"Then it is settled," Vakama announced. "Begin your tale, Onewa, for we are turned to hear."

Onewa smiled. "And well you should be. My story begins in the vast, frozen region of Ko-Wahi, on a very different night from this. A night when it seemed that all was lost for the Toa and Mata Nui itself . . ."

ONEWA'S TALE: THE MOUNTAIN

When Kopaka Nuva, the Toa of Ice and protector of the Village of Ko-Koru, is troubled, he travels to a remote spot on the slopes of Mount Ihu to think. The only sound is the wind rushing through the mountain passes and the crunch of ice beneath his feet. Even other Ko-Matoran rarely go there, so no other living being interrupts his time alone.

Most of the time.

"Brother!" Pohatu's voice boomed across the snowfield. Somewhere in the distance, an avalanche started by his shout roared down the mountainside.

Kopaka turned and saw the powerful form of the Toa of Stone struggling to walk through the hip-deep snowdrifts. It was tough going for one as heavy as Pohatu. He no doubt needed help making it through.

Without a word, Kopaka resumed walking up the icy pathway.

"I know you can hear me!" Pohatu shouted. Kopaka narrowly dodged the rain of icicles shattered by that sound.

"Mata Nui can hear you, and he is sleeping," Kopaka muttered.

Down below, Pohatu watched as his brother Toa continued slowly and steadily up the mountain. Walking through snow was almost as bad as being underwater. Then again, Pohatu supposed snow did combine the worst parts of Gali's realm with those of Kopaka's. Still, he was determined to reach his destination, with or without the help of the Toa of Ice, and although he wore the Great Mask of Speed, Pohatu hesitated to use it. On this slippery surface, running would not get him there any faster.

Pohatu continued to follow Kopaka through the darkness, doing his best to ignore the cold. In turn, Kopaka ignored *him*, hoping he would turn back. Sometimes that worked with Pohatu, but not often.

"Help! Brother, help me!"

Kopaka whirled and saw Pohatu floundering in a drift. The Toa of Po-Koro had lost his footing and gone down. Without something solid to hold on to, Pohatu was finding it impossible to rise.

Frowning, Kopaka split his ice blade in two and attached the ends to his feet. In an instant, he was flying down the mountain on his power ice-skates, sparks flying as the protodermis blades sliced through the ice. He was aiming for the curved lip of a ridge, and as always, his aim was true. His momentum sent him soaring through the chill air toward Pohatu.

Kopaka waited until he was at the height of his arc, then curled up and did a series of midair flips. He hit the slope at just the right angle and slid to a stop beside the fallen Toa.

"I will help you up," Kopaka said, as quietly as a snowfall. "Then you will leave my land."

"I have a better idea," replied Pohatu, springing to his feet. "I'll get up on my own, thanks, and then we'll travel together."

"You faked your fall."

"Oh, no, brother, the fall was real . . . tricky things, these snowfields," said Pohatu. "I welcomed the rest. And while I was lying there, I thought, *Trying to get to Kopaka is really quite tiring. If I stay here, perhaps he will come to me.*"

"There is a blizzard coming. With my ice powers stolen by the Bohrok-Kal, I will not be able to stop it," said Kopaka grimly. "Turn back."

Pohatu folded his mighty arms across his chest. "Here I am, and here I'll stay."

Kopaka shrugged. "Very well. When I reach Ko-Koro, I will tell Turaga Nuju to have you dug out when the thaw arrives . . . if it ever does." With that, he turned and walked away.

Pohatu frowned and hurried after him. "I thought we could help each other. There are many masks to find. Don't you remember how well we worked as a team when we first arrived on Mata Nui?"

"You buried me in a landslide, as I recall," said Kopaka.

"Oh. Well, I didn't do it on purpose. Besides, that can't happen now. I've lost my powers, just like you have."

Kopaka stopped dead and looked over his shoulder. "Pohatu, I do not want your help. I do not need your help. I will find the Kanohi Nuva on my own."

Before Pohatu could answer, Kopaka had vanished into the darkness. The Toa of Stone stared after him for some time. Then he started to follow again, careful to stay in Kopaka's footsteps.

The blizzard that struck was one of the fiercest ever known in Ko-Wahi. The winds roared down from the summit of Mount Ihu, carrying blinding snow and stinging pellets of ice. In moments, every trace of Kopaka's passage had vanished beneath the drifts.

Pohatu stopped to think. He knew his brother Toa was following an ice path, but where was it? If he began digging through the snow to search, he would freeze long before it could be found. Unless . . . unless he could find a new use for the Mask of Speed.

Doing his best to ignore the subzero temperatures and the blowing snow, Pohatu planted his feet on the ground. Then he held his arms out in front of him and began to rotate them, faster and faster, letting the power of the Mask of Speed, Kanohi Kakama Nuva, flow through him. In seconds, his arms became a blur as they sent twin blasts of air before him, which blew the snow aside to reveal the hidden path.

"Let's see Kopaka do that," Pohatu said to himself as he resumed his journey.

Kopaka had more to worry about than the snowstorm. When his elemental powers were stolen, his resistance to extreme cold disappeared as well. For the first time, he could feel the numbing temperatures of the Ko-Wahi region slowing him down. All he wanted to do was rest, preferably someplace warm. He would lie down and sleep, only for a few moments, in the shelter of a rock outcropping. Then he would be ready to resume his search for the masks.

The cold and the darkness were closing in on him. In icy dreams, he saw two of the insect-like Bohrok-Kal, Kohrak-Kal and Nuhvok-Kal, stealing the symbol of his Toa power from his village. His energy was gone. He could hear them shouting his name, over and over, and something else . . . a terribly familiar growl.

Kopaka awoke with a start. Standing over him, saliva dripping from its jaws, was a Muaka. The largest and fiercest predator in Ko-Wahi, the great cat saw anything that moved as prey. Its claws dug into the icy floor as it sniffed Kopaka, trying to determine if the Toa was still alive and might be a threat.

Once I would have been far more than a threat, Rahi, Kopaka thought, using the Matoran name for a wild animal. *Two days ago, a single ice blast from my blade would have left you frozen solid. But today it is just a powerless tool and little defense against a beast of such power. The Bohrok-Kal have stolen all my Toa energies.*

It was then that Kopaka heard his name shouted again. That was no dream. It was Pohatu, still searching through the snow for his brother Toa. Better still, it was enough to distract the Muaka just long enough for Kopaka to roll away, grab his blade, and sprint toward the mountainside.

The Muaka bellowed and pursued, its long legs easily making up the ground between them. Kopaka could just see a narrow ledge high on the rock face. If he could reach it, he would be safe, since it was too high for the Muaka to reach. But somehow he doubted the Rahi would give him the chance to climb.

There was no time to plan. Kopaka broke into a dead run, holding his ice blade in both hands. He could feel the Muaka's breath on his back. His feet were slipping underneath him, and he knew any fall would be his last.

Eyes locked on the mountain, Kopaka counted down the seconds. He would get one chance to make this work. If he failed, Ko-Koro would need another protector. *So I will not fail,* he said to himself.

Before the Muaka could react, Kopaka planted one end of his ice blade into the ground and vaulted high into the air. He struck the mountain hard and began to slide down the ice-covered rock. He was slipping off the ledge, with the Muaka waiting below, jaws open wide.

Something whizzed past him, burying itself in the rock with a loud metallic sound. Kopaka reached out and grabbed it. It was one of Pohatu's climbing claws! Down below, the Muaka snapped at the Toa's heels. With his last bit of strength, Kopaka hauled himself onto the ledge.

The Muaka snarled and leaped, scrambling in vain to hold on and then sliding back down to the snow. It was preparing for another try when the sharp crack of rock striking rock caught its attention. The sound repeated three times before the Muaka decided it might mean easier prey and loped off to investigate.

As soon as it was gone, Pohatu appeared. "I

might not still command the rock," he said, "but at least I can still toss one."

Kopaka yanked the climbing claw free and tossed it to the Toa of Stone. "I thought you had turned back, Pohatu."

"I was going to," the Toa said, shrugging, "but mask hunting alone is like playing the sport of kolhii alone — good practice, but not much fun."

Kopaka slid down into a snowbank and approached. When he spoke, his voice had a bit less ice in it than usual. "You should go home, Pohatu. This is no place for you . . . perhaps not even for me, anymore."

"Turaga Onewa said something to me before I left Po-Koro," replied Pohatu. "He said it's easy to be a hero when you have plenty of power and your only worry is whatever enemy is fool enough to challenge you. It's not so easy when all you have is your wits and your biggest enemy is yourself."

The eyepiece of Kopaka's mask extended and whirred as he scanned the mountainside. "That sounds like Onewa. You two are much like the stone you represent. Solid. Practical. Down-to-earth."

"Well, thanks, I —"

"Dense. Hardheaded," Kopaka continued. "And stubborn."

"You're welcome, Kopaka," Pohatu snapped. "Oh, no, rescuing you was my pleasure."

Kopaka glared at his brother Toa. "If your trick had failed, the Muaka might have had us both. The strength of the Toa would have been reduced by one-third and our villages would be in peril. Foolish risks are a luxury we cannot afford."

Pohatu pointed up the mountain. "Then maybe we should get out of the way of the avalanche!"

It was too late to react. A wall of white slammed into the two Toa, knocking them both off their feet and carrying them along in its wake. Helpless, they tumbled end over end down Mount Ihu, bashing into rocks and almost losing their Kanohi. Kopaka made a desperate effort to will the avalanche away, but not even the slightest trace of his powers remained.

Toa of Ice and Stone wound up sprawled in a heap at the base of the mountain, half buried in snow. Long minutes passed before they staggered to their feet, exhausted and aching. "I hate winter," Pohatu growled.

"The Mask of Shielding would have protected us from that," Kopaka said. "We need to find the Kanohi Nuva now. As long as you are here, Pohatu . . . you might as well travel with me."

"It's certainly been fun so far," the Toa of Stone replied, brushing snow from his arms and legs. "Onewa mentioned a Mask of Shielding in an ice cave near here. Any idea where that might be?"

Kopaka did not answer. He stepped away from Pohatu and activated the power of his mask, enabling him to peer through tons of stone into the network of caves within Mount Ihu. It was the work of moments to find a cavern in which there was a lone Kanohi Hau Nuva, the Mask of Shielding.

"It is nearby," he reported. "Perhaps half a kio up the mountain. But the entrance is —"

Before Kopaka's eyes, Pohatu vanished,

only to reappear a split second later. "Blocked by boulders. I know. I saw," the Toa of Stone said. "Mask of Speed, remember?"

Kopaka's eyes narrowed and his voice was like sleet striking a suva shrine. "Don't do that again."

Pohatu was tempted to argue, but the storm was growing worse. Neither Toa could see more than a short distance ahead. They walked together in an uncomfortable silence, fighting the wind and the snow as they made their way back up the mountain.

Finally, though, it was too much for the Toa of Stone. "What's the matter with you, brother? I rescue you, you aren't pleased; I scout ahead to save time, you aren't pleased. Is there no pleasing you, Toa of Ice?"

Kopaka stopped and said, "I am not here to be pleased. I am here to find Kanohi Nuva so I can regain my stolen powers and truly be the Toa of Ice again. If you wish to help, fine. If you wish to talk . . . seek out Toa Lewa."

Not another word was spoken by either.

*   *   *

The cave mouth was not a pleasant sight. The entrance was blocked by massive boulders that had fallen sometime during the night. Even Onua Nuva, Toa of Earth, helped by his Mask of Strength, would have had a difficult time clearing them all away.

Kopaka set to work trying to pry the stones free with his ice blade. But the tool was not designed for that type of work and he soon gave up in frustration. Pohatu, meanwhile, had done little but stand to one side, observing.

"Difficult," Kopaka said.

"No, no," answered Pohatu. "Simple. Watch me."

Pohatu approached the pile of stone and gently laid his hands upon it, first on one spot, then another. He almost seemed to be listening to the rock, though how he could hear anything above the howl of the winds, Kopaka had no idea.

"It's a puzzle, brother," said Pohatu. "Each stone supports another. Alone, they are powerful. Together, even a Toa cannot budge them. But the key to the puzzle is there, if you know how to look."

"Where did you learn this?" asked Kopaka.

Seeing that his brother Toa was genuinely interested, Pohatu smiled. "Onewa taught me. He said that his knowledge of rock is older than the rocks themselves. Not quite sure what he meant by that, but it certainly sounds impressive. Ah! Here we are."

Pohatu drew back his leg and slammed a center stone with a mighty kick. The rock splintered and flew apart. Robbed of their support, the other stones collapsed, revealing the cavern entrance.

"See? When they can't work together and share the burden, they can't perform their task."

For just the briefest instant, Kopaka almost smiled. "Yes, brother. Perhaps I do see."

Kopaka led the way into the ice cavern with Pohatu close behind. The Toa of Ice carried a lightstone, its glow reflecting off of the polished surfaces of the cave. The only sounds were their breathing and their heavy footsteps on the ice.

Pohatu lost track of how far they walked. He was beginning to wonder if they would be able to find their way out again, then reminded himself that Kopaka's Mask of X-Ray Vision would show the way. He felt uncomfortable here, with so much ice cutting him off from the feel of stone.

Their progress was halted by a great crevasse that yawned in the cavern floor. Pohatu crouched and peered into the gap. "It's blacker than Makuta's spirit down there, brother. No telling how far it goes."

"We will find out," said Kopaka. "The Kanohi Hau is at the bottom."

Pohatu sighed. "Someday I am going to have a long talk with whoever hid these Kanohi," he said, checking to make sure his climbing claws were well fitted.

Kopaka split his ice blade in two, taking one half in each hand. They would not be as efficient as Pohatu's claws, but they were strong enough and sharp enough to serve as climbing spikes. He scanned the crevasse again, satisfied that there was nothing down there but the mask, and nodded to Pohatu. "We begin."

Pohatu rammed a claw into the ice wall and swung his legs over the edge of the gap. "I hope Mata Nui appreciates all this, if he ever wakes up."

The climb down was slow and treacherous. Once one of Pohatu's claws slipped, and only fast action by Kopaka kept the Toa of Stone from plummeting to the floor far below. By the time they reached the bottom, both Toa were exhausted.

The gray Mask of Shielding, the Kanohi Hau Nuva, was wedged in a far corner, perhaps a hundred kio away. Its power would protect a Toa from any physical attack, provided it was not unexpected. Of all the Great Masks, it was perhaps the most valuable to possess now, when the Toa were without their elemental energies.

Kopaka took a step toward the mask, but Pohatu grabbed his arm. "Hold it, brother! Do you feel that?"

"What?"

"I am not one with the earth like Onua, but something is wrong . . . very wrong."

Suddenly a violent earth tremor struck the mountain, shaking it like it was a toy in the hands of a Matoran. Pohatu looked up in time to see the roof of the cavern far above collapsing, sending tons of rock and ice plunging toward them.

Pohatu didn't hesitate. He rammed Kopaka hard with his shoulder, sending the Toa of Ice flying across the icy floor toward the Kanohi. Kopaka slid to a stop against the wall, an arm's length from the mask. Stunned, he looked up to see half the mountain about to crush Pohatu.

Kopaka scrambled and grabbed the mask, slamming it onto his face. The Hau Nuva mask had the power to protect those near the wearer as well. If he was in time, the shield might extend to Pohatu. If not . . .

The shield flared to life around Kopaka. Stone rained down upon it and shattered to harmless fragments, while the ancient energies of the Kanohi kept the Toa of Ice safe. But there was no sign of Pohatu.

It felt like an eternity before the quake ceased. Kopaka scrambled over the rubble toward where Pohatu had last been standing and began to dig with his hands. "Pohatu! Pohatu!" he shouted, but the only answer was the echo in the cave.

In the end, he was forced to give up. Nothing stirred beneath the rock.

"Good-bye, my brother," Kopaka said. "Perhaps we were too different to truly be friends. But a noble heart beat within that body of stone."

Grimly, he turned from Pohatu's final resting place and began the long journey back to the surface.

A full day passed before Kopaka reached the village of Po-Koro. Matoran lined its newly constructed walls, on the alert for any appearance of the Bohrok-Kal. The approach of the Toa of Ice sent a stir through the guards, for all knew he rarely ventured out of Ko-Wahi these days.

Turaga Onewa met him at the gate. "You journey alone, Kopaka, in this dangerous land?"

"No," replied Kopaka. "I journey with the memory of a fallen brother." He handed Onewa the Kanohi Hau Nuva. "This belongs here. Without Pohatu, it would never have been found . . . nor would I be alive to carry it. He died as he lived, a true hero."

"I thank you for that, brother!" The booming voice came from behind Kopaka. All who saw him that day would later say that the Toa of Ice was not so cold as some believed. For he turned with a smile to see the approach of Pohatu, battered and weary but very much alive.

"Pohatu! It is good to see you once more," Kopaka began. Then he swiftly added, "I mean, it is good to know that Po-Koro will not be left undefended in this time of danger."

"Thanks to you," said Pohatu. "The power of the Mask of Shielding protected me, but not before I was stunned by the falling rubble. Still, it enabled me to survive the quake and your efforts made it easier for me to dig myself out. Too tired to climb, I walked until I found a tunnel that led to another, and so on. I emerged in Onu-Koro and made my way here."

Kopaka took the Hau Nuva from Onewa and handed it to Pohatu. "This is yours. Although I believe your courage is a greater shield than this mask could ever be, Toa of Stone."

"I will take the mask anyway, brother, with gratitude," replied Pohatu. "For I believe we will need every bit of power — and all of our courage — to make it through the days to come."

WHENUA'S TALE: THOSE WHO FORGET THE PAST . . .

His tale finished, Onewa sat down with a smile. "So you see," he said, "Kopaka's refusal to accept help could have led to disaster. After all this time, has he learned nothing about unity?"

Nuju clicked and gestured furiously. Matoro translated, "The Turaga says Pohatu was too stubborn to leave when asked. He should have respected Kopaka's wishes."

"Seems to me neither was too everquick," Matau put in. "But the Kanohi was discovered-found, was it not? And now they are true brothers-friends."

Vakama nodded. "That is true, Matau. They

are both very brave. But do they have the wisdom to understand what has gone before?"

"I will tell my tale," Turaga Whenua said softly. "And then we shall see."

Toa Onua Nuva dove to avoid the flailing tentacle of the massive subterranean worm. The dead-white appendage narrowly missed him, smashing into the tunnel wall with such force that the whole place shook.

The Toa of Earth had heard of these creatures before but thought they were only Matoran legend. Those who mined protodermis, the substance of which everything on Mata Nui was built, had occasionally spoken of great tentacled worms that lived in the very deepest tunnels of Onu-Wahi. Some claimed they ate protodermis and were attracted by the piles of ore gathered by the workers. One thing no one argued was that the appearance of such a creature was more than enough to shut down a mine for good.

Now I see why, Onua said to himself. *If that thing weren't blind, it would have caught us long ago.*

The Toa looked over to see how his companion was managing. Turaga Whenua was doing his best to hold off the creature with his drill, but without actually doing it any harm. Unfortunately, that meant his efforts were not having much effect.

"I think we are going to have to subdue this beast," Onua suggested, rolling out of the way of another blow. "Not that I can imagine how."

"No!" Whenua said. "This creature has existed on Mata Nui longer than either of us. He is a link to the past. He must not be harmed!"

Onua grabbed a tentacle as it went by, trusting to the power of the Great Mask of Strength to hold it steady. The worm simply tossed him aside as if his strength were no more than an annoyance.

"A shame the beast does not feel the same way about us," said the Toa. "Our past he may be, but we will have no future if we do not defeat him!"

A few days before, stopping the creature would have been no problem for Onua. With his command of the earth, he could have raised a wall of dirt and rock to protect himself and Whenua. But when the Bohrok-Kal stole his Nuva symbol, he had lost his power — perhaps for good.

The Turaga leaped over a swinging tentacle and landed next to Onua. "Think, Toa of Earth, with something besides your Great Mask! Force is not the answer."

So Onua dodged, and rolled, and thought. He remembered his decision to seek out a Kanohi Kaukau Nuva said to be hidden far below the surface. Over his objections, Whenua insisted on coming along. They had been journeying for more than a day, through tunnels long abandoned by the Matoran, when they encountered the worm.

Whenua dodged another wild swing and shouted, "Think! What do you know about this creature?"

Not enough, thought Onua. *It's big; it's strong; it's bleached white, like so many other creatures of the underground; it lives in constant darkness, so it is blind and navigates by . . .*

Hearing!

Despite the danger, Onua managed a smile. It all seemed so simple, once the truth was stumbled upon.

Working quickly, he used his twin quakebreakers to carve two huge stones out of the rock wall. "Guard yourself!" he shouted to Whenua as he brought the two boulders together with a mighty crash.

The explosion of sound echoed through the tunnels, leaving even the Toa of Earth deafened and stunned. The worm let out a roar of anger and withdrew into the darkness below, far from the source of that horrible noise.

Whenua was speaking, but at first Onua could not hear him. After a short time, the ringing that filled his mind quieted and he was able to make out the Turaga's words. "So," said Whenua, "you found his weakness."

"Yes. He makes up for his lack of sight with supersensitive hearing," said Onua. "So it was a reasonable guess that he would hate loud noise."

"Guess? Bah!" snapped Whenua. "It was no

guess. It was knowledge gained from your experience of the realm of Onu-Wahi. It was the past speaking to you."

Onua said nothing. Of all the Toa, he was the best at not speaking unless he had something worthwhile to say. Only Kopaka lived in greater silence, by choice.

"Come," said Whenua, continuing down the tunnel. "We still have far to go, Toa of Earth."

Later, the Toa and the Turaga sat in a small cavern and shared a meal from their packs. Even Onua, who had spent most of his existence beneath the surface, could not remember having been down this deep. He wondered what waited below, as well as what adventures his brother and sister Toa might be having far above.

"They will be fine," said Whenua, almost as if he were reading the Toa's thoughts. "They can be strong, as long as they do not forget the source of their power."

"You mean the Kanohi?" asked Onua.

"No, I do not mean the masks. I mean true power — the power of six Toa, side by side."

Onua frowned. It had not been so very long ago that the Toa of Fire and Ice, with support from the Toa of Air, had suggested the Toa Nuva part ways. Gali had protested, but he himself had said nothing. Afterward, she was angry with him for his silence. He had questioned ever since whether he had chosen the right path.

"The decision was made to pursue our own destinies," he said. But he could not manage to make the words sound believable, even to himself.

"You have but one destiny," said Whenua. "You owe it to the past . . . to the Toa who have gone before you . . . to see that destiny through."

It took a moment for the Turaga's words to sink in. *The Toa who went before us? What is he talking about?*

When he turned to ask, Whenua was already gone.

*   *   *

He caught up with the Turaga around the next corner. The tunnel sloped sharply downward here and the air was warmer. Onua wondered if they were still in Onu-Wahi, or if they could have journeyed as far as the realm of Tahu. It certainly felt like they were in the heart of a volcano.

When he pressed Whenua for an explanation of his words, the Turaga shook his head. "I meant nothing. Besides, we have far greater things to worry about than that right now."

At first, Onua did not know what he could be talking about. Then he remembered that the Kanohi Ruru mask Whenua wore gave the Turaga far greater night vision than even the Toa possessed. Now that he looked harder, he could see the floor and walls up ahead were . . . moving.

Despite the oppressive heat, the Toa of Earth suddenly felt very, very cold.

"Kofo-Jaga," he whispered. "Fire-scorpions."

Whenua took a step backward. "Alone, no threat. But in a swarm . . ."

Onua nodded. In a swarm, Kofo-Jaga could bring down a creature many times their size.

They thrived on heat and flame, and although they plagued Onu-Wahi, many believed they were native to the lava pits of Ta-Koro. Certainly they would follow the scent of molten magma wherever it might lead.

"We have to turn back," said Whenua. "They have not noticed us yet."

"Run?" Onua replied in disbelief. "From an insect?"

"You are very wise, Onua," said the Turaga of Earth. "Perhaps the wisest of all the six Toa. But experience is the greatest teacher. What does experience tell you?"

Onua respected his Turaga, admired him, and would have given his life to protect him. But he still hated it when Whenua was right.

"Fire-scorpions felled a full-grown Kane-Ra bull, a hundred suns past. It was a day the beast still remembers with pain," said Whenua. Then he added, "He was too foolish to know to avoid them."

Onua Nuva did not answer. He simply turned his back on the Kofo-Jaga and walked away.

*   *   *

"I came with you to see what you have learned from the past," said Whenua as they continued their journey. Onua had not spoken a word since the encounter with the fire-scorpions.

"And what is the lesson I am learning today?" the Toa asked bitterly. "That without my earth power, I must flee from the smallest creatures on Mata Nui?"

Whenua stopped in his tracks. "To be a Toa is to defeat all who oppose you?" The Turaga held up a clenched fist. "Is this what you believe a Toa to be? A mighty arm to strike down your enemies?"

"No. But our power —"

"Is nothing. A Toa's true strength is here," Whenua said, pointing to his head. Then he placed a hand over his heartlight, saying, "And here. Your Toa power can move the dirt. . . . Your mind and heart can move mountains."

Whenua began to walk again, Onua beside him. "And is that what you used when we met the Kofu-Jaga?" the Toa asked.

"My mind told me they have a sting,"

Whenua replied. "My heart told me I would not enjoy it."

They followed the tunnels deeper and deeper into Mata Nui. The farther they went, the hotter it became, until the walls were too searing to touch. Even a Ta-Matoran, who farmed lava all day and surfed it all night, would have turned back by now.

More than once, Whenua had to stop to catch his breath. Onua waited patiently, not wanting to risk getting separated from him. There was no telling what might live this far under-ground.

"One day, I will walk along a beach in Onu-Wahi," the Toa said at one point. "And I will spot a Kanohi Mask hanging from a tree. I will pluck it like a fruit and my search will be done."

Whenua laughed. "Yes. The same day Makuta decides he would like a little sun, and perhaps a friendly game of kolhii."

"Why are the masks so hard to find? If we are meant to have them —"

"You are meant to *earn* them, Toa of Earth. That is the answer."

Onua stopped and held out a quake-breaker to block Whenua's progress. "Hold, Turaga. Do you hear that?"

Whenua could, indeed, hear something, but wished he did not. It was the harsh, ugly sound of massive claws snapping. He did not need his Noble Mask of Night Vision to know the source.

"The chamber of the mask is just ahead," he whispered. "But, like fish to a reef, the presence of a Kanohi has drawn the Manas."

Onua and Whenua edged closer, their backs flat against the hot tunnel wall. The sight that greeted their eyes made both regret having such keen night vision. Two giant Manas crabs clashed in a huge chamber, striking at each other and then scuttling away, only to strike again. Both were easily three times the size of the Toa, and infinitely more powerful. Beyond them, the Kanohi Kaukau Nuva rested on a rocky outcropping.

"Makuta's guardians," said Whenua.

"They were," corrected Onua. "We Toa

defeated them and drove them away. But it took the six of us, merged into the mighty Toa Kaita, to do it."

"When they cannot fight others, they fight among themselves," said Whenua. "Before you came to Mata Nui, none had ever seen them and returned to tell the tale."

Onua slumped against the wall, not even noticing the intense heat now. The powers of six Toa combined had barely been enough to defeat these creatures before. How could one Toa, stripped of his elemental energies, hope to win? It was hopeless. . . .

Whenua winced as one of the Manas just narrowly missed the other with a snapping pincer. "Too big to slip by. Too fast to avoid. If only the other Toa were here . . ."

"Even if the others were near, they could only delay those beasts, not defeat them," Onua said sadly. "I can see no way to . . ."

Whenua turned and looked up at the Toa of Earth. Onua was silent, staring intently at the Manas, his quake-breaker resting against the wall.

His eyes glowed like twin points of flame in the darkness.

"I have been looking ahead," Onua said, more to himself than to the Turaga. "I need to look behind."

"What are you talking about?"

Onua didn't answer. He had his quake-breakers running at full speed and was boring holes, seemingly at random, in the walls. Blasts of superhot air greeted him each time.

"What are you doing?" Whenua demanded. "Have you lost your mind?"

"No," Onua answered, not pausing a moment in his work. "I have begun to think like a Toa."

"Like a Toa who has lost his mind," grumbled the Turaga. "It isn't hot enough down here for you?"

Onua plunged his quake-breaker deep into the stone, then drew it out again. The tool glowed red-hot. "It is. It is hot enough for the Manas as well."

"Hot enough for . . . ?" Whenua glanced at the great crabs. They were still absorbed in their contest against each other. He thanked Mata Nui for the favor.

"When the Toa Kaita faced the Manas, we defeated them with intense cold," Onua said, grinding more holes in the stone. "Manas hate the cold. They fled down here to be where it's hot."

Whenua stared at him but said nothing. Onua obviously had a plan, but the Turaga could not imagine what it might be. *Looking behind,* he said. . . . Whenua sifted through his memories, but he could find nothing that explained this strange behavior. Still, it was not the first time he had questioned the wisdom of a Toa, and he had been wrong before.

Onua noticed Whenua's puzzled expression from the corner of his eye and laughed softly. "Come now, Turaga. You, who always say I should not forget the past? Think — what else do we know that loves the heat?"

As he said this, Onua found what he was seeking. His quake-breaker burst open a lava pocket and molten magma began to pour into the tunnel, heading slowly but surely for the

Manas' chamber. Whenua leaped high in the air and wrapped his arms around the Toa's neck.

"Of course!" he proclaimed happily. "I should have remembered myself. But will it work?"

"If it doesn't, I do not think we will return to tell about the attempt," replied Onua. "If the lava doesn't get us, the Manas most certainly will."

The Toa calculated there was little time. The lava was seeping closer and closer to the Manas. As soon as they noticed its approach, they were bound to spot the Toa and Turaga and charge. If he had been wrong about what other creatures might be living in this furnace . . . or if it took them too long to reach here . . .

"Onua! They are coming!" Whenua shouted, pointing back up the tunnel. Now Onua could hear the *skritch-skritch-skritch* of a thousand insectoid legs scrambling over stone.

The Kofo-Jaga were on the march.

Drawn by the heat and the scent of lava, they swarmed down the tunnel. Onua and Whenua flattened themselves against the wall to let the insect horde go by. Just as the fire-scorpions reached the chamber, the Manas saw the molten lava closing in on upon them. They roared in anger, snapping at the magma tide, backing away toward where the Kanohi waited.

If the lava was too much for the Manas, it was like a warm bath to the Kofo-Jaga. But they had no intention of sharing their good fortune. First by the thousands, then by the millions, they moved toward the Manas, fiery stingers ready to challenge their new enemies.

The Manas were creatures without fear, but not to the point of stupidity. Little by little, they gave ground before the swarm, clearing Onua's path to the mask. Their claws flashed as they struck at the fire scorpions, but it did no good. There were simply too many of the Kofo-Jaga.

"It must be now!" Onua said. Then he charged into the chamber, ignoring the lava, the fire-scorpions, and the angry Manas. Before the creatures could react, he snatched the Kanohi from its resting place and dove for the tunnel entrance.

Whenua watched, wide-eyed, as the Toa of Earth headed right for him on a collision course. "Mata Nui!" the Turaga shouted, jumping aside just in time to avoid being tackled.

Onua Nuva struck the tunnel floor quake-breakers first, carving his way through the stone and vanishing through it. Five seconds later, Whenua heard a splash from far below.

The Turaga rushed to the ragged edge of the hole and peered down. There was Onua, the Kanohi Kaukau on his face, treading water in a subterranean river. "Turaga! Jump!"

Whenua took another step toward the edge, then dizziness washed over him. Heights were for Le-Matoran, not the Turaga of Onu-Koro. "I cannot!" he shouted back. "It is too far!"

The Toa of Earth smiled. "Turaga Whenua, remember the past," he said. "Haven't I always caught you before?"

The river carried them far from the Manas and the Kofo-Jaga to the mouth of a wide tunnel. Once they were back on dry land, Onua shifted from the Great Mask of Water Breathing to the Great Mask of Strength. Together, they began the long trek up to the village.

They had been walking only a short time when Whenua paused, running his hand over the tunnel wall. Onua could see faded Matoran letters carved into the stone just below the ceiling, but too much time had passed to read what they said.

"What does it mean, Turaga?" he asked.

"The past," Whenua said, with wonder in his voice. "I carved these letters long ago . . . the same day I carved this tunnel."

The Turaga said nothing further. But he wore a smile all the way back to Onu-Koro.

MATAU'S TALE: THE TRAP

Whenua wore the same smile as he finished his story. "You see, Onua remembered the past even when I did not. The Toa are wise . . . wise enough to understand."

"You trusted your Toa, and he trusted you," Onewa replied. "But do they trust one another?"

Vakama glanced at Onewa, then at Matau. "Our brother of stone speaks the truth, though I am sorry to say it. There is little friendship left among the Toa, it seems."

"Do not be so quickjumping, Vakama," Matau, the Turaga of Le-Koro, answered. "There is much you do not know. Let me tell my tale of Toa and trust. . . ."

* * *

Lewa Nuva, Toa of Air, stood at the edge of a cliff overlooking the lush domain of Le-Wahi. Hidden in the jungle below was his village, Le-Koro, only recently rebuilt after being leveled by the Bohrok.

He shuddered a little at the memory. The day the insectlike Lehvak swarm succeeded in sweeping away the village was the same day they captured him, removed his Mask of Power, and used one of their parasitic krana to make him one of them. He could have resisted, of course, but the Lehvak had already taken over Turaga Matau and the Le-Matoran. Challenging the Bohrok might have placed his friends in danger.

He closed his eyes and did his best to drive the memories away. For a brief time, his mind had been filled with thoughts that were not his own. They were the voices of the swarm, commanding him to help them complete their task on Mata Nui. Had it not been for Onua's timely rescue, Lewa knew he might still be a servant of the Bohrok.

It had taken him a long time to feel

comfortable after that. The other Toa, particularly Tahu, treated him differently. Some felt sorry for him; others seemed nervous that he might turn against them. Now, when he finally felt like the old Lewa again, his power over air was gone. Once more, as he journeyed through this land he knew so well, he felt lost.

That was what had brought him to the cliff. In the days since his power disappeared, he had not attempted to glide on the air. Before, he could command the wind to keep him flying. Now it would not listen to him. Wisdom said he should keep to the trees and the vines . . . or worse, walk on the ground! But the day he did that, he knew, would be the day he stopped being a Toa.

He fitted his twin air katana onto his arms and legs, turning them into glider wings. The breeze was right. If all went well, he would soar over the jungle and land in the heart of Le-Koro. He took a step forward. . . .

"Toa Lewa!"

Startled, Lewa almost fell. He fought to

keep his balance, not easy with the glider wings in place. Then a hand grabbed his and pulled him back from the edge.

It was Turaga Matau, looking concerned. "Word is deepwood that you are seeking Kanohi Nuva Masks. There are no power-masks here. Only mountain-rock."

"I know, Turaga," said Lewa. "But I have been treebound for too many suns now. It is time to ride the wind again."

Matau laughed. "Is this a day for sunsoaring? Very well, then. You will find your Toa-brother on the groundpath below. Try not to hardland on him."

Another Toa in Le-Wahi? Yes, now that Lewa thought of it, there was something new in the wind. The scent of . . . smoke.

"Yes, and hot-fire, too," said Matau. "Enough to darkash Le-Koro again, if someone does not stop it."

The Turaga said the words lightly, but there was no mistaking their meaning. Le-Koro was in danger again. No matter the cause, Lewa would not fail his village a second time. He stepped to the edge of the cliff, took a deep breath, and launched himself into the wind.

At first, he had a hard time holding steady. Gusts blew him about like a leaf, up above the mountain and then down almost to the treetops. The smell of fire was much stronger now, but Lewa still could not see any flames.

He shifted his body to try and turn right. The wind had other ideas, blowing him toward the left and into a spiral toward the ground. By instinct, he tried to summon the air currents to carry him high again. But the air would no more listen to him these days than it would to Gali or . . .

Tahu!

Of course. It must be the Toa of Fire down below. If smoke was in the wind, did that mean he had somehow regained his powers? Lewa had to know. There was no more time for testing his flying. He triggered the power of the Mask of Levitation and floated gently to the ground.

Lewa did not like being on the flat earth.

Yes, it was better than being in the water, which he positively hated. But he always felt clumsy when he "groundwalked," not like when he was swinging through the trees.

Lewa loped along the path, following the scent of fire. He could hear the crackling sound of the flames feeding on old branches. He hoped it was not the trees of Le-Koro that were burning.

Coming around a rock, he saw Tahu. The Toa of Fire was standing in front of a blaze, magma swords in hand. Lewa recognized his stance. Tahu was trying to stop the fire by drawing the flames into his swords, but it was not working. His power, too, was gone.

Lewa rushed over to him. At first, Tahu did not seem to notice the other Toa. Lewa had to grab his arm to get his attention. "Tahu! Trying to quickburn the jungle, Fire Toa?"

Tahu shook him off. "Toa of Fire? Toa of nothing! I no longer command the flames, Lewa."

A small group of Le-Matoran scurried into the clearing and began shoveling earth on the fire to put it out. Lewa led his brother Toa away. "We all face the same hardluck, Tahu. But it's no time for angershouts. Why have you come to Le-Koro?"

Tahu looked at the Toa of Air. He had always liked Lewa, even if their ideas about being a Toa were very different — Lewa saw it as fun and adventure, Tahu as a serious task. But so much had changed in the last few weeks: Lewa taken over by the Bohrok, the Toa Nuva splitting apart, now the loss of all their powers. Tahu was no longer certain what — or who — he could trust.

"It is . . . not your concern, brother," replied Tahu. "I will not be in your region long. Once I have what I have come for, I will be on my way."

"If you search for something in my lands, then a wayfinder you must have," said Lewa brightly. "And a wayfinder I shall be. Turaga Vakama has told you where a mask can be found?"

"Two," said Tahu, already walking away. "I would welcome your company, Toa of Air."

That way I can keep an eye on you, the Toa of Fire added to himself.

*   *   *

Of all the regions of Mata Nui, Le-Wahi was easily the most difficult to travel through. The air was heavy with rain and the ground was mostly mud. The farther one went into the heart of the wahi, the denser the jungle growth became. Even for Toa, hacking through vines every step of the way was exhausting.

However, if Tahu and Lewa were tired, the sight that met their eyes in the center of the swamp was enough to wake them up. A grove of trees had been torn out of the ground, roots and all, and piled on top of one another to block the path.

An even worse surprise waited when Tahu tried to lift one of the trees. Even without the Great Mask of Strength, a Toa should have been able to toss a swamp tree aside. But this one felt like it weighed twice as much as Mount Ihu. After three tries, Tahu gave up.

"Nuhvok-Kal has been here," he said. "This is its work."

"How could a Bohrok-Kal do this?"

"It controls gravity, Lewa. First it makes the

trees so light that they float out of the ground . . . then so heavy that they crash to earth and cannot be moved. You, of all Toa, should know that."

Lewa stiffened. When he spoke, the normally light tone of his voice was gone, replaced by anger. "No. I did not choose the Bohrok dark-time I lived through. I do not know where the Bohrok-Kal are or what they are doing."

Tahu leaned in close until their masks almost touched and said harshly, "How do I know that? How do I know your 'wayfinding' is not leading me into an ambush?"

"If I were your enemy, you would be lateknowing. Better to worrythink about the Nuhvok-Kal."

Tahu frowned. He could not help being suspicious of Lewa, whose mind had so recently been controlled by their enemies, the Bohrok. None of the other Toa knew that Tahu, too, had once lost a mask and had it replaced with a krana. Although he had not worn it long enough to be absorbed into the swarm, he knew how powerful the krana could be. Sometimes the Toa of Fire worried that his decision to split up the team might have been caused by the Bohrok somehow.

"All right, then," Tahu said, backing off. "The Kal knows we need the Masks of Power, so it's probably heading for the same spot we are. We find it; we capture it; and we make it give our powers back."

Lewa began to scale the barrier, climbing effortlessly over the stacked trees. "You are heartfeeling, brother, not headthinking. Nuhvok-Kal is not so easy to capture. Take one step toward it and you are highflying or ground-bound."

Tahu began to climb, but it was not quite as easy for him as it had been for Lewa. Once he slipped and almost fell back to the bottom, which did nothing to improve his mood. "Do you have a better idea, Lewa? Perhaps if we ask the Nuhvok-Kal to give us back our Toa powers, it will agree to think about it."

"Think about it . . . ?" Lewa repeated. Then he jumped from the top of the barrier, went into a roll on landing, and leaped up into a tree. "Mata Nui! What a quicksmart idea, brother!"

Tahu reached the top of the barrier and looked at Lewa as if his brother Toa had turned into a giant swamp lizard. "I am beginning to wonder, Lewa, if the Toa of Air has too much of it inside his head. What idea?"

Lewa was now springing from one branch to another almost faster than the eye could follow. "Have you ever seen a Nui-Jaga at a bog snake nest?"

Tahu shook his head. He knew that the giant, scorpionlike Nui-Jaga liked to feast on bog snakes, but he had never witnessed it. He swatted aside a swarm of insects and snapped, "No, and what does that have to do with anything?"

"Nui-Jaga very hugebig," answered Lewa from high atop a tree. Then he jumped off, flipped over and over, and landed on a lower branch. "Bog snakes are many, but small. So what to do when hungry Rahi comes around?"

Lewa dropped to the ground in front of

Tahu. "Bog snakes come from in front, behind, up-tree, downtree, all at once. Nui-Jaga gets confused. Too many for even sharpstinger to stop. Understand now?"

Tahu had to admit that this was a rare case where he did understand exactly what Lewa was saying.

The two Toa began to plan. Lewa sent a message back to Le-Koro, instructing Turaga Matau to gather as many vinesmen and windriders as possible and send them to the Toa. Meanwhile, Tahu went to scout ahead and see if he could spot the Nuhvok-Kal.

When he returned, Lewa was already putting the Matoran to work. The green-masked villagers were up in the trees all around, tying off branches, readying rocks, and rigging nets made of vine. Tahu was impressed.

"They work hard, brother. You should be proud of them."

Lewa smiled. "They learn from lifedawn

that he who climbs fastest and highest will get the sweetest fruit. And . . . they have special reason to want any Bohrok stopped."

Tahu looked around. Of the dozens and dozens of trees that surrounded the clearing, not one was empty. Even if no Matoran was visible, the rustle of branches said one was at work turning the jungle into a giant Bohrok-Kal trap.

The idea was a simple one. Nuhvok-Kal was incredibly powerful, but all power has some limit. Come at the Kal from different directions, like the bog snakes do the Nui-Jaga, and make it use its power again and again. With luck, it would reach its limit. If not . . .

"What happens if this doesn't work, Toa Tahu?" The question came from Kongu, one of the Le-Koro Matoran.

"It has to," Tahu replied.

"It will," said Lewa. "Now we just have to lure the Nuhvok-Kal to this spot."

"We will need some clever trick," said Tahu. "Some bait it cannot resist."

Lewa turned to the Toa of Fire with a broad smile. "Make sure you shoutloud so the Kal can hear you, brother."

Nuhvok-Kal was angry. Its mission was to find and free the trapped queens of the Bohrok swarms, and it wanted to be doing that. But Tahnok-Kal had ordered that the Kanohi Nuva masks be found and hidden so the Toa could not use them.

Nuhvok-Kal had been searching for the masks since first light, with no luck. It did not like the jungle. Too many places for enemies to hide. Not that anything on this island could threaten a Bohrok-Kal.

"Creature!" boomed the voice of the Toa of Fire. "Turn and face justice for your deeds!"

Nuhvok-Kal wheeled around to see Tahu, magma swords drawn. Far from being a frightening sight, the Kal would have laughed if it were able. Instead, its harsh voice hissed, "Toa Tahu! I thought I smelled the scent of failure somewhere nearby."

"Then perhaps you should bathe more often, Bohrok," Tahu replied. "Are the powerful Kal now searching the jungle for scraps? Or are you just lost?"

The Kal didn't respond with words. Instead, it lifted its shield and sent waves of gravitic energy at the Toa of Fire. Rocks and trees, freed of the bonds of gravity, began to float into the air all around Tahu. Slowly, they drifted together until they were hovering just above the Toa's head.

Tahu flipped backward a split second before Nuhvok-Kal increased gravity by a hundred times. Stone and wood slammed into the ground where he had been standing, coming down so hard they buried themselves deep in the mud.

The Toa of Fire scrambled to his feet and shouted, "Follow me, Bohrok! Perhaps we can find more rocks for you to throw!"

Then Tahu raced away, heading for the clearing where Lewa waited. He knew Nuhvok-Kal was following, for he could feel his legs growing heavier with each step. If the Bohrok-Kal got any closer, its power would root Tahu to the ground and the plan would fail.

The Toa of Fire's only chance was the unexpected. He raced up a slope, leaped, and grabbed a tree branch. He spun around the branch to build up momentum. At the peak of his motion, he let go and shot forward like a Matoran disk.

He almost missed the vine he was shooting for, grabbing it at the last moment. Tahu swung out over the jungle, letting go of one vine only to grab another. He could hear trees falling behind him as the Bohrok-Kal continued the chase.

One final swing brought Tahu into the clearing. Halfway through his arc, he let go and landed hard in the mud. Lewa rushed over, not sure whether to be stunned or amused at the sight of the Toa of Fire as a vineswinger.

"Don't say a word," Tahu warned.

"I wouldn't thinkdream of it," said Lewa, trying hard to hide a smile. "Everything is ready."

"Good. It's right behind me."

The two Toa split up, each rushing to a different side of the clearing. The Nuhvok-Kal burst through the trees a second later, shouting, "Toa! You cannot escape from the Bohrok-Kal!"

Lewa thrust his air katana into the air. "Now!" he yelled, and chaos was unleashed.

From all around the clearing, Matoran slung disks and stones and branches, all aimed right at the intruder. Nuhvok-Kal reacted by reflex, using its power to erase gravity from each and every object thrown. But even as they floated toward the sky, more came to replace them. The Bohrok-Kal spun around frantically, trying to keep track of everything coming its way.

Lewa waved to get Tahu's attention. "Brother! I can quicksteal his krana-kal!"

Tahu shouted, "No! Wait!" but it was too late. Lewa had already broken into a run, leaped . . . and went crashing to the ground when Nuhvok-Kal's power struck him. He lay at the Bohrok-Kal's feet, pinned to the ground by the crushing weight of gravity.

Tahu started forward to rescue him . . . then paused. What if Lewa was still being controlled by the Bohrok? What if this was all a trick? Could he trust a Toa who had been a part of the swarm such a short time ago? The whole trap had been Lewa's idea . . . but who was meant to be caught in the snare?

All of this ran through the Toa of Fire's mind in an instant. His answer came to him even more quickly. He could not — would not — turn his back on a brother Toa, no matter what.

He charged. Nuhvok-Kal turned to face him and unleashed his devastating power. But Tahu was already gone, leaping and spinning in the air, striking the falling stones with his magma swords. One rock crashed into another, sending it hurtling into a third, all moving too fast for even the Bohrok-Kal's eyes to follow. No sooner did the Kal send its power against one stone than it was ricocheting off of three more, all scattering in different directions.

In all of this, Lewa was not forgotten. Tahu hit the ground, grabbed the Toa of Air, and carried him to the safety of the trees. "Stay here!" he ordered. "I will deal with the Kal."

But Nuhvok-Kal had had enough. As Lewa had predicted, the constant rain of rock and wood and the effort to stop it all had exhausted the Bohrok-Kal's power. It stumbled into the jungle, using its last reserves to bring trees down behind it to slow pursuit.

Tahu started after him, but Lewa called, "Wait, Tahu. Let it go. There will be another clashtime to settle with the Kal."

The Toa of Fire wanted to argue . . . but hadn't he just realized he had to trust Lewa? He turned back and said, "You may be right. Are you ready to travel? We have Kanohi Masks to find, after all, my brother."

Together, the two Toa headed into the jungle, Tahu walking, Lewa swinging through the trees. "How can you groundwalk, Tahu, now that you have vineswung?"

"I leave the trees to you, brother. And if you ever tell anyone about that, I'll —"

"Our secret," answered Lewa. "Heartswear. But next time, work on that hardland, brother. . . ."

Then the Toa of Air's laughter could be heard all over Le-Wahi . . . and the Toa of Fire's, too.

NOKAMA'S TALE: BENEATH THE SURFACE

Vakama laughed, his whole body shaking. "Tahu swinging through the trees? No wonder he was in such a foul mood when he returned to Ta-Koro that day."

Nuju ran through a complicated series of gestures. Matoro translated, "Perhaps it did the Toa of Fire some good to see the world the way Lewa sees it."

"They have been good Toa brothers since then," said Matau. "All doubtfear is gone, it seems."

"Perhaps, Matau," said Onewa. "But if we make the wrong decision . . . if we tell the Toa all that has gone before . . . then won't they 'doubtfear' us? We have kept this from them for so long, why would they ever trust us again?"

Nokama rose to her feet. "Brothers, I know what it is to betray a Toa. I have done it, and not so very long ago. Listen to my tale, and I beg you not to judge until I have reached an end."

The Turaga fell silent as the Turaga of water began to speak . . .

Hahli rowed her canoe frantically through the bright blue waters of Gali's Bay. She ignored the schools of Makuta fish that pursued the boat, despite the fact their jaws could easily tear the craft to pieces. Nothing mattered but finding Turaga Nokama.

She beached her boat on the outskirts of Ga-Koro and raced up the sand. Macku was on the beach, repairing a seaweed fishing net. "Have you seen the Turaga?" Hahli asked.

Macku could see how upset her kolhii ball partner was and put down her work. "Yes, she is inspecting the work site. What's the matter?"

"I'll tell you later," Hahli said, on the move again. "I have to talk to her!"

She found Nokama up on a ridge, supervising a Ga-Matoran work team. A Bohrok squad had tried to build a dam to cut off the waters that fed the bay, until Gali drove them off. Now the Matoran were tearing down what was left of the structure.

"Nokama! You have to come quickly!"

The Turaga turned and saw Hahli. The Matoran was out of breath. "What is it, Hahli? Calm down and tell me."

"It's Gali Nuva. I saw her on the beach, and this huge wave came at her. . . . She raised her aqua axes . . . but she couldn't stop it! Her power over water is gone!"

Nokama frowned. She suspected something like this might happen when the Toa Nuva symbol was stolen from the village. "Where is Toa Gali now?"

"Still on the beach, last I saw," said Hahli.

"Stay here. I will go to her. She will need someone who understands."

Nokama arrived on the beach to find Gali stalking up and down, her aqua axes tossed aside like they were worthless fish bones. The Turaga had never seen her so angry before.

"Gali? Are you unharmed?"

The Toa of Water's eyes flashed. "I cannot hear the water. I am deaf to the song of the waves, Nokama, the ebb and flow of every river and stream on Mata Nui. I walk this island, but I am no longer a part of it. No. I am not unharmed."

Nokama bent down and picked up the aqua axes. "Your Toa tools are not to blame."

"No, my brother Toa are," Gali snapped. "I told them we should stay united. I told them there would be another menace and we would be stronger together. But Tahu and Kopaka would not listen . . . not even Onua stood with me."

Nokama handed the tools back to the Toa. "And will raging like the storm change that? Be at peace, Toa. Remember, calm waters are the easiest to travel."

Gali walked away and sat down on a rock overlooking the bay. "With respect, Turaga, that is easy for you to say. You do not know what this feels like."

Nokama laughed softly. "You are so wise, Gali, yet know so little. You are swimming in my wake, Toa. There is nowhere you can go that I have not traveled before."

Nokama walked to the water's edge and dove into the bay, swimming with long, easy strokes. "One day I will tell you a tale, and you will understand. But for now . . . come with me."

Another world exists far beneath the waters of Mata Nui. Here schools of fish congregate around protodermis reefs, feeding on the microscopic organisms that dwell within. Then, without any warning, the school compresses itself into a tight cluster, in a desperate attempt to defend against a Takea shark on the hunt. One pass, two, and the cluster is shattered, fish darting every which way in a race for safety.

Gali had seen this many times in her travels under the sea, but never before had she understood how vulnerable the fish must feel. *It is bad enough the Bohrok-Kal menaced the island, but if Makuta should return . . .* The thought filled her with fear. Without their elemental powers, the Toa Nuva would stand as much chance against the master of shadows as those little fish had against the shark.

The Toa of Water forced herself to focus on the present. Nokama was swimming quickly, leading Gali deep into the night-black waters near the bottom of the bay.

The journey ended in a sea cave, one Gali could not recall ever exploring. Inside she discovered that the cavern held air pockets. The atmosphere was heavy and stale, but breathable just the same. A large lightstone embedded in the wall illuminated the entire cave.

"Why have you brought us here? What is this place?" Gali asked.

"It is a place of memories," Nokama replied. "Look."

Carved into the stone were six figures, each wearing a Kanohi Mask and carrying a strange tool. They did not look familiar to Gali, but there was no mistaking the fact that these were Toa.

"Who — ?" she began.

Nokama gestured for her to be silent. "Who they are . . . or were . . . is not for you to know right now. But they are one reason you are here. As for the other reasons, you will find a Kanohi Nuva in this cave . . . and a test as well."

"A test? Why, Turaga?" Gali demanded. "After all the Toa have achieved on Mata Nui, why must we still be tested?"

"When you know the answer to that, Toa Gali, you will have passed the test," answered Nokama, already swimming out of the cave. Gali pursued, but a huge stone slab suddenly slammed down, blocking the cave mouth. She threw all her might against it, but it would not budge.

The Toa of Water was trapped. The only thing worse than that was knowing that she had been betrayed by the one she trusted most.

Outside of the cave, Nokama let go of the ancient stone lever that triggered the slab. In her heart, she wished there had been another way. But Gali would need true wisdom in the time to come, and not every lesson can be taught by a Turaga telling stories. Some only life can teach.

I hope Gali can forgive me . . . if she ever finds her way out, thought the Turaga.

Gali treaded water and tried to think. There would be time later to learn why Nokama had done this. Right now, she needed to find a way out.

She thought about the other Toa Nuva and how they would approach this problem. Onua and Pohatu would rely on brute strength and try to smash the slab. Lewa would see the whole thing as another reason to hate water. Tahu would probably order the slab out of the way, and if it knew what was good for it, the slab would move aside.

And Kopaka? The Toa of Ice always said, "The trap itself contains the key to escape. You simply have to know where, and how, to look."

All right, Kopaka's way it is, then, she said to herself. *Assuming Nokama is not being controlled by Makuta, she wanted me to find something or learn something here. But what?*

Gali took a deep breath and forced herself to be calm. Once all worry and fear were gone, she looked around her, trying to take in every detail. The cave walls were smooth — too slick to climb. Running a hand over one, she noted that it was not the uneven texture caused by years of erosion. These walls felt like they had been polished. This was no natural sea cave, then. It was more like an Onu-Wahi tunnel.

The only other remarkable feature seemed to be the carvings. Gali swam closer to take a good look at them. They were very old, made long before she or the others had come to Mata Nui. The Toa pictured were definitely not her brothers or herself, but something about them did look familiar. It took her a moment to realize it was the Kanohi they wore. The masks were not like any she had seen before, but somehow she knew what they were. And one of the Toa looked like . . .

No, it couldn't be, she told herself. *I must be mistaken.*

Seeing the Kanohi made her realize that she had forgotten the most important clue Nokama had given her. There was a Mask of Power hidden somewhere in this cave. Finding it must be the test, and once she had it, she could escape.

Gali dove beneath the water and began to swim deeper into the cave.

The Toa of Water swam slowly, surfacing now and then to get her bearings in the unfamiliar cave. She had seen schools of Ruki minnows, cut off from the open sea, flitting about in the water in search of escape. Strangely, though, there did not seem to be any larger fish. Didn't anything live down this deep?

Further exploration answered her question. Through the murky water she spotted bones littering the cavern floor. She retrieved one and brought it to the surface to examine it in the glow of the lightstone. It took her only an instant to remember where she had seen such a bone before: Nokama's trident. These were Makuta fish bones.

Suddenly, Gali felt very alone and a little bit afraid. Makuta fish were certainly prey for larger creatures, like Takea, but few made any effort to hunt them down. Makuta fish were fast and cunning, with rows and rows of razor-sharp teeth in their mouths. Although any one was powerful enough to survive on its own, they preferred to swim in a school. Together, there was little that could stop them.

Much like the Toa, Gali thought.

But something had defeated the Makuta fish. Something strong enough and fearless enough to challenge them. Gali hoped that, whatever it was, it had abandoned this particular cave long ago.

She looked down the tunnel, but saw nothing that looked like a threat. Just the glow of two lightfish hovering in the water, waiting for their dinner to swim by. Gali wondered if there wasn't something in the waters beyond them, much larger and much nastier, waiting for exactly the same thing.

Gali continued her journey, scanning beneath the waters for any sign of a Kanohi. She saw none. Against her will, she began to wonder if Nokama could have been lying about the mask. Then she pushed that thought aside.

The two lightfish had still not moved the slightest bit, despite her drawing closer to them. Normally, even a good-sized fish would startle at any movement. Of course, they probably had never seen a Toa before.

Don't worry, little ones, Gali thought. *The Toa of Water will not harm you.*

As if in answer, the lightfish suddenly went out. A second later, they began to glow brightly again.

Gali froze.

Lightfish never stop glowing, not while they are alive. Which meant those weren't lightfish.

They were eyes. And they had just blinked.

Gali spun around and hurled herself forward, trying to go back the way she had come. But it was too late. She felt a tentacle wrap around her right leg, then another around her left. Despite all her power, she was being slowly dragged backward.

The Toa of Water looked over her shoulder. The creature that had her in its grip was a monster with twelve enormous tentacles. Each tentacle had a snapping beak on the end, and another, larger beak could be seen in the center of the creature's body. Its eyes glowed brightly as it pulled Gali closer and closer.

Desperately, she looked for a way out. Fighting the creature was a last resort, she knew. She had no wish to harm anything that lived, and besides, there was no guarantee she could overpower something this size.

Another tentacle was reaching toward her now, trying to wrap around her waist. Using all her strength, Gali dove toward the cavern floor, narrowly avoiding the creature's grasp. She planted an aqua ax into the stone floor, trying to slow her progress toward the creature. Her free hand reached out for something, anything, to hold on to.

Then she felt the familiar shape of a Kanohi Mask. She had found it! Gali grabbed it and put it on, immediately feeling the speed power of the Kanohi Kakama flowing through her.

Her joy turned to disappointment. She had been hoping it would be a Pakari Nuva. Greater strength would help her wrestle herself free. What good was speed when she was held in such a grip?

Worse, without the powers of the Mask of Water Breathing, she could stay under for only a brief time before she needed air. If she was going to put the Kakama to use, it had to be now.

She remembered something Tahu had once said. "Fire never surrenders," he had told her. "If it cannot burn through, it burns around. Block its path and it sends sparks through the air, to begin the blaze anew somewhere else. Fire always finds a way."

Can water do less? Gali asked herself. Then she began to kick her legs, faster and faster, until they were nothing but a blur. Still, the creature would not let go. She increased her speed, straining for air as she forced her legs to move even faster.

In a test of sheer strength, Gali could not win. But even stripped of her elemental energies, she could still be saved by the power of water. Her ultrarapid kicking generated a current stronger than any ever seen before in the waters of Mata Nui. It slammed into the creature with the force of a tidal wave, rocking it just enough for its grip to loosen. Gali seized her chance and rocketed forward. In a split second, the tentacled monster was left far behind.

The Toa of Water shot through the cavern, carried forward by her momentum. She could feel some of the familiar effects of the Mask of Speed. Her reflexes had become lightning quick, the only thing making it possible for her to maneuver at such high speed. Her vision was sharper. Objects that should have been just a blur were sharp and clear to her.

Unfortunately, that also meant she could see what she was heading for: the slab Nokama had lowered over the cave mouth. Now that she had the Mask of Speed, Gali could look forward to being flattened against the stone that much faster.

No! Water finds a way!

The Kakama Nuva was more powerful than the old Mask of Speed. Maybe it could do more than just make her swim more quickly. She had to concentrate . . . concentrate on getting through that stone.

Gali drew on her last bit of energy and willed her body to begin to vibrate. Every atom in her body began to move until she was nothing but a blur moving through the water toward the slab. If she had guessed wrong, she would be crushed against the stone by her own speed.

Seconds before she was to strike the stone, the Toa of Water shut her eyes. Her final thoughts were of the other Toa. She wished her last words to Tahu and Kopaka had not been such harsh ones. Even more, she wished she could be by their side to confront the dangers to come.

Then the thought hit her — at the speed she was going, she should have reached the cave mouth by now. Cautiously, she opened her eyes. She could see sunlight filtering through the water high above, Ruki fish darting everywhere, even a lone Tarakava lurking close to the shore. She was back in the bay.

Gali called the Mask of Water Breathing back to her and turned back to look at the cave. The slab was intact. Somehow, her vibrations had allowed her to pass right through the stone without injury. The Mask of Speed had been even more powerful than she expected it to be.

She thought of the carvings, Nokama's "test," even her differences with Tahu and Kopaka. And she wondered how many of those things were also far more than they seemed.

* * *

When Gali broke the surface, Nokama was standing on the beach waiting for her. The Turaga smiled and held out a hand. "Welcome home, Toa of Water."

Gali waited a moment, then took the outstretched hand and stepped out of the water. "You wanted me to discover the Kanohi Kakama's powers on my own. You wanted me to see they were no longer the same as before."

"Nothing is the same," Nokama replied. "The Toa have changed. Your Kanohi have changed. You may soon find that everything you think you know about Mata Nui, about your life here, is but a fraction of the truth."

Nokama stopped and looked up into the Toa's eyes. "You are the Toa of Water, Gali. You, above all, must be able to look beyond the surface and find the hidden depths below."

Gali considered Nokama's words as they walked along the beach. When she spoke again, it was to say, "Those carvings in the cave . . . was that you, Turaga?"

"Me?" Nokama laughed. "Now, Gali, did you see a Turaga in that picture? Those were Toa. Heroes of a long-ago age. I am just the elder of Ga-Koro."

Yes, *you are*, thought Gali. *But what lies beneath your surface, Turaga?*

NUJU'S TALE: PLACE OF SHADOWS

Nokama looked around at the other Turaga. With the exception of Whenua, all of them looked as if she had just suggested building a temple to Makuta.

"Those Toa carvings should have been covered up years ago," said Vakama. "Showing them to Gali without talking to the rest of us first was most unwise."

"Why? Because I do not like asking Toa to risk their lives for us again and again while lying to them about the past?" replied Nokama.

"Nokama speaks the truth," said Whenua. "Listen to her."

"I have been listening," said Onewa. "I have yet to be convinced these Toa will understand the tales of Metru Nui. It seems they barely understand one another."

Nuju gave a shrill whistle and ran through a complicated series of gestures. Matoro translated, "Sometimes accepting what you do not understand is the first step toward understanding. Hear Nuju's story and decide for yourselves. . . ."

Gali Nuva stood on Kini-Nui in the twilight, remembering. It had not been so very long ago that she and the other five Toa had emerged from the Bohrok nest, changed by protodermis into the powerful Toa Nuva. At first, it seemed like a blessing. Their greater strength and tougher armor would make it easier for them to defend the village from any threat.

But as they began to test their new power, the team began to fracture. Finally, Tahu and Kopaka almost came to blows. Before she even knew what was happening, the two of them had decided the Toa should go their separate ways. Each Toa would pursue his or her own destiny, all thoughts of unity forgotten.

At first, she had dismissed the Toa of Fire and Ice as foolish and stubborn and vowed not to ally with them again. Now her talk with Nokama had convinced her that perhaps she was the one being stubborn. Gali decided she had to try to bring the Toa back together.

Her meditation was interrupted by the arrival of Kopaka. "Hahli sent word that I was needed," said the Toa of Ice. "So I am here."

"Thank you, Kopaka. I knew you would not refuse my summons."

The Toa of Ice said nothing. He looked uncomfortable, but then he often did around Gali. She had always insisted on treating him as a friend, even when he insisted he did not want or need friends.

"It concerns the Kanohi Nuva Masks," she said. "As soon as one other arrives, I will explain."

Kopaka's eyes narrowed. "Another? Who?"

"It is I, Toa of cold breezes!" The voice belonged to Tahu, who vaulted onto the Kini-Nui to stand beside them. "You can go back to your snow fortress. I am sure Gali and I can handle matters."

Kopaka smiled. "Perhaps, if all Gali needs is water boiled."

"I sent for both of you!" Gali said sharply. "Tahu, kindly stop acting like you are Mata Nui's gift to us all. Kopaka, for a Toa of few words, you never seem to know when to be quiet."

"I did not come here to be lectured, sister," Tahu replied. "I have business in Ta-Koro, and —"

"We three have business right here, Tahu. Masks of Power are waiting to be found, but I cannot find them alone. And neither can either of you."

Gali looked from one Toa to the other. "Now, do we help one another . . . or do we let our pride do to the Toa what Makuta could not?"

There is an old Mata Nui legend about a horned lava rat from Ta-Wahi forced to ride on the back of a Takea shark to make it across a stretch of water. They were not very good traveling companions. The rat worried that the Takea would eat him, the shark that the rat would burst into flames at any moment, as lava rats are known to do. It made for a very quick and very tense trip.

The three Toa making their way along the border of Ta-Wahi and Ko-Wahi made the rat and the shark look like the best of friends. Kopaka had not spoken more than two words since they left Kini-Nui. Tahu, on the other hand, had not shut up. Gali was wishing she could have her powers back for only a few seconds so she could summon a cold rain for them both.

"Lewa, of course, was worried about what the Nuhvok-Kal might do, but I knew it would flee before me," said Tahu. "After that, finding the masks was a simple matter."

"So you have said," commented Gali. "Twice."

"In Ko-Koro, they call it 'whistling past Makuta's lair,'" said Kopaka.

"What's that, Toa of slush?" asked Tahu.

"You tell your tales to keep your courage warm, Tahu," the Toa of Ice replied. "What better use for hot air?"

Tahu's hand went for his magma sword. Gali stepped in between the two Toa. "Enough! We have reached our destination."

Tahu and Kopaka turned to look. The three Toa were standing at the beginning of a narrow path that wound between the mountains. The Toa of Fire was not familiar with the site, but Kopaka knew it well.

"The 'place of shadow' — that is what the Matoran call it," he said. "Even the Bohrok avoided this spot. Is this where the masks are to be found, Gali?"

"Three of them, or so Nokama tells me. But there is great danger here, as well."

"You have the Mask of Speed," said Tahu. "Why don't we just race in, retrieve the masks, and race back out again?"

"Too easy to speed into a trap," Gali answered. "No, we must make this journey one step at a time. Be on your guard, Toa, for we know not what waits for us within."

* * *

The sun was shining when the three Toa began their trek. It did not take them long, however, to learn how this spot had gotten its name. They were barely on their way when the mountains seemed to close in around them, cutting off all light. The brightest of days turned into the long shadows of dusk in an instant. The warm breezes of Ta-Wahi were gone now, replaced by an icy wind that chilled them to the core of their beings.

No one spoke as they walked. In this place, a whisper would have seemed like a shout. All around was cold, hard stone, without so much as a weed growing amid the rocks. There were no sounds, for nothing dared to live here.

Kopaka led the way, sharing the power of the Mask of X-Ray Vision with his two companions. In spite of this, they *heard* the danger long before they saw it. It was the rumble of thunder, so loud it shook the ground, and the howl of the wind that almost drowned out their thoughts.

Gali pointed overhead. Black clouds now filled the sky, where a moment before it had been clear. Twin lances of lightning flew from those clouds, striking the peaks and shearing off huge chunks of stone. Boulders flew down the mountainsides heading right for the three Toa.

"The Mask of Shielding will protect us!" Tahu yelled over the wind.

"No!" Kopaka shouted. "It will protect us from being crushed, but not buried! We need the Great Mask of Strength!"

Tahu started to argue, but Gali stopped him with a look. He summoned the Great Mask of Strength, sharing his powers with Kopaka and Gali. All three felt a surge of energy in their bodies as their strength increased.

"Spread out!" Gali said. "We need room to move!"

As the boulders rained down, the Toa struck with their tools, crumbling tons of stone to powder. Without a shield to protect them, even one stone getting through could mean doom. Tahu, Kopaka, and Gali struck blow after blow, swatting away massive rocks as if they were hailstones.

Above, lightning bolt after lightning bolt struck the mountains. Rocks that had taken an aeon to rise to the sky were sent tumbling to the ground in a flash. Only the reflexes and power of the Toa kept them from being overwhelmed.

When the avalanche finally ended, all three sank to the ground, exhausted. "What was that?" Gali asked.

"A welcome from the shadows, perhaps," answered Kopaka.

"We have to keep moving," said Tahu. "We can't let a few pebbles stop the Toa."

Kopaka used his ice blade to help himself to his feet. "You are right."

Gali looked up at the Toa of Ice, surprised. "Did you actually agree with him?"

"You do not need the wisdom of a Turaga to know that if we stay here, whatever lurks in this place will know where to find us," said Kopaka. "We need to move on."

"Come on, Gali," Tahu said, helping her up. "This is your expedition. You wouldn't want to miss the next narrow escape, would you?"

*   *   *

Tahu took the lead this time, while Gali hung back to talk with Kopaka. "You know Tahu does not mean all he says, Kopaka. But so many look to him as a leader, and to him that means he can never ask for help."

"Then that is the difference between us," Kopaka replied. "He cannot ask for help . . . and I don't need it."

But Gali was no longer paying attention. Her eyes were locked on the path up ahead and her expression was one of shock. "You may want to change your mind about that, Kopaka."

The Toa of Ice followed her gaze and saw Tahu, swords drawn, standing before a raging wall of fire. "Toa of ash! What have you done?"

Tahu did a backflip away from the advancing flames. "It was not my doing, brother. It erupted from the ground like lava from the Mangai. Perhaps your icy breath can blow it away?"

"Perhaps you both can stop acting like quarreling Makika toads and pay attention!" said

Gali. She pointed to a second wall of fire that had appeared behind them. "We cannot go forward, and back is not looking very appealing, either!"

"Up?" suggested Kopaka.

"At the speed these fires move, we would never make the climb in time, brother," said Tahu.

Waves of heat washed over Gali and the world began to spin around her. She reached out to steady herself on Tahu's shoulder. "Brothers . . . the heat . . . too much . . ."

Kopaka looked at Tahu. "You know the ways of fire. If we cannot go over or under . . ."

"Then we go through," agreed Tahu. "Gali! We need the powers of the Mask of Speed!"

"Yes . . . of course . . ." Gali said, struggling to stay conscious. With great effort, she summoned forth the Kanohi Kakama Nuva.

Tahu took her left hand, and Kopaka her right. With a final glance at one another, the three Toa launched themselves at the fire at top speed. Running so fast their feet barely touched the ground, they broke through the flames and emerged on the other side, unharmed.

"You see? At such speed, even the fire could not touch us," said Tahu proudly.

"No . . . no, there is something wrong here," Gali muttered. She stumbled back toward the fire, reaching out to touch it. Kopaka rushed forward to stop her, but she brushed him aside.

"Gali! No!"

Tahu's cry came too late. Without a moment of hesitation, Gali plunged her hand into the flames. But no cry escaped her lips, and when she drew it out again, it was not even scorched. "It's not real. None of it. It's a trick."

At first, Kopaka and Tahu thought perhaps Gali had broken under the strain of lost powers and the long trek. But they both knew the Toa of Water too well. They could hear the absolute certainty in her voice, and so they believed her words. As soon as they accepted them as truth, the flames vanished.

"We have seen this once before, in the Bohrok tunnels. We thought it was the Bahrag's work," said Gali, her voice grim. "We were wrong."

"Makuta," Tahu whispered.

"Striking at us through our minds," said Kopaka.

"We turned away from unity. When we did that, we turned from our duty and destiny as well," said Gali. "In that moment, we became vulnerable to Makuta."

"But no more!" thundered Tahu. "Now we know he sends nothing but illusions at us. And illusions will not stop the Toa of Fire! Come, we will find those Masks of Power! We will make Makuta regret ever hearing the name Toa!"

Without waiting for a yes or no from his companions, Tahu marched off. Gali and Kopaka followed behind, walking quickly to keep their brother in sight. "At least we know now we cannot be harmed, as long as we do not believe in the illusions," Gali said.

"Yes," replied Kopaka. "There is only one problem. What if the next danger . . . is no illusion?"

* * *

Darkness brought their journey to a temporary halt. Gali had the unique privilege of watching Tahu and Kopaka work together to start a fire. Once it was blazing, Kopaka went off to stand guard while the other two rested.

Gali was the first to break the uncomfortable silence. "Kopaka tells me Pohatu is well."

"As is Lewa," said Tahu. "Of Onua, I have heard nothing."

"It is not right that we should be so uncertain of a brother's safety. We were meant to stand together, Tahu, as one."

"But we are six," he replied. "Six Toa, each with enough power to defeat any menace . . . or at least, we once had such power. And we will have it again!"

"Yes. Then we will go our separate ways again, avoiding one another's wahi, until some new threat rises to strike in the borderlands. That is the price we pay for the pride of fire and ice."

"Water," Tahu said, as if it were a curse. "Water soothes and calms and lulls the spirit to sleep. You cannot understand what true power demands."

Gali's eyes blazed with anger. "Toa, if the Great Beings see fit to restore my energies to me . . . I may one day show you what power really is."

Tahu stood and walked away, saying over his shoulder, "The prophecies may say that we have to work together, sister. But nowhere is it written that we must enjoy it."

The next day dawned bright and clear, but a shadow still lay over the Toa. Gali and Tahu were not speaking to each other. Kopaka spoke to neither, not out of anger, but simply because he saw no need to clutter the morning air with words.

They had gone only a short distance when Gali called a halt. She had spotted a carving on the rock wall. It showed the six Toa she had seen before, this time in a valiant struggle against . . .

what? It might have been some many-armed sea creature, or perhaps some other Rahi they had never seen before. One thing was certain — they were in a place of fire.

"Impossible!" said Tahu. "If such beings ever roamed Ta-Wahi, I would know of it."

"As we knew of the Bohrok, brother?" asked Kopaka quietly. "Or the Kal?"

"What are you saying, bringer of winter?"

"Simply that the Turaga hold many secrets. Perhaps too many."

Gali said nothing, but her thoughts were on her earlier encounter with Nokama. What did they truly know about the Turaga? Was any of it the truth?

She did her best to ignore her doubts as they journeyed onward, but it was not easy. As one of her brothers had once pointed out, there were too many unanswered questions about Mata Nui. Perhaps when the Bohrok-Kal were defeated, it would be time to get some answers.

"There!" Tahu shouted. He was pointing up ahead, where three Kanohi — the Great Mask of

Strength, the Great Mask of Levitation, and the Great Mask of X-Ray Vision — sat atop stakes planted in the ground. Although a dull gray when not being worn, still the Pakari, Miru, and Akaku gleamed in the sunlight.

"Perhaps our worries were for nothing," said Gali. "Our enemy has fled. Nothing guards the masks."

"Nothing that we see," corrected Kopaka. "Even with my enhanced vision, the way seems clear."

Strangely enough, it was Tahu — normally the boldest of Toa — who hung back. "Something is not right here. When have we ever found Kanohi so easily? This is another trick."

Kopaka focused the power of his Kanohi Akaku on the masks. "They are real. No illusion."

"I understand your caution, Tahu," said Gali. "But we do not have time to waste. If the masks are there to be taken, we must take them."

Reluctantly, Tahu nodded and joined his two companions. Perhaps Gali was right. Perhaps whatever had been placed here to guard these masks had fled. With a final glance at Kopaka and Gali, he reached out to take the Miru.

The next instant, they were plunging into darkness, falling end over end into what seemed like a bottomless well. Tahu had noticed too late that the ground was giving way beneath them. There was no time to grab on to the edge or dig his magma swords into the walls. All he could do was fumble with the Miru and hope the Mask of Levitation would do its work.

The Kanohi did not disappoint. As soon as the mask was on his face, Tahu could feel himself floating gently in the air, held aloft by the power of levitation. Kopaka and Gali, too, were safe thanks to the power of the Nuva mask.

They reached the bottom, finding themselves in a cold, dark chamber far beneath the surface. All three were on alert, but Gali was the first to say, "We are not alone here."

"No, brothers, you are not." Onua stepped out of the shadows, followed by Pohatu, Lewa, and Turaga Vakama. "It seems the Toa Nuva are together again, if not in the way we would have wished."

"Who is responsible for this?" Tahu raged. "The Kal? If so, I will —"

"No, Toa," said Vakama. "Even the power of the Kal could not tame what lives in this place. It is a menace I hoped never to face again. Even at the height of your powers, you could not hope to defeat it . . . only contain it."

Kopaka frowned. "Another secret, Turaga? What is this thing we face?"

A deafening roar filled the chamber. Each Toa drew his or her tools and looked around, but there was nothing to see.

"What is it, Toa of Ice? A thing of raw power . . . a creature with no fear. It was created for only one purpose, and one alone."

The fear on Vakama's face was clear to see in the glow of his firestaff. "It lives to defeat Toa."

VAKAMA'S TALE: SECRETS

Vakama stood, his eyes on Nuju. "That is enough. I will tell the rest of this story. After all, I was there."

"Yes, you were," said Nokama. "But neither you nor Nuju have told us about this before now. Why?"

"I asked Nuju to keep his silence," answered Vakama. "But now the time has come to tell the tale."

The six Toa Nuva took up positions around the chamber, their eyes fixed on the entrance to the darkened tunnel. From somewhere in those shadows came the roar of the creature Turaga Vakama swore no Toa could defeat. But the heroes of Mata Nui had no intention of giving up without a struggle.

"I will bait the beast," Tahu said. "The rest of you close in on it from behind. We may fall, but by the Great Beings, this creature will know it has faced Toa!"

"Tahu, think," Gali implored. "We have the Masks of Speed and Levitation. We can escape this chamber the same way we did the lair of the Bahrag — flight!"

Kopaka shook his head. "We could, Toa of Water — if not for that," he said, pointing to the ceiling.

The hole through which they had fallen was gone now, replaced by dozens of sharpened stalactites. Even with the enhanced strength granted by the Kanohi Pakari, the Toa could never get safely past all those spikes.

"All right. Then we stay here," Gali said firmly. "And we make sure someone regrets it."

The guttural growl came again, closer this time. Onua, closest to the tunnel entrance, could hear the sound of massive claws scraping against stone. "What is this thing, brothers? Nothing could be as large as it sounds."

Tahu glanced at Vakama. "Well, Turaga, you said you know of this creature. We are in great danger — isn't this usually the time you reveal your secrets?"

Vakama stared straight ahead. His eyes never wavered from the tunnel as he whispered the words of an ancient text from memory. "Beware the Rahi Nui . . . beware the beast of horns and claws, who stalks land, sea, and air. Born to seek the Toa, it will bring down all the works of Matoran in its path. You will know it by its roar, by the shaking of the ground as it strides, by the fierce glow of its eyes. Guard well against it, or it shall be the end of all."

When he had finished speaking, he lowered his firestaff to his side and stared at the ground. None of the Toa could recall ever seeing Vakama look so defeated.

"Well, those were cheerhappy words," Lewa commented, sarcasm in his voice. "I thought perhaps this beast was something to worry-brood about."

"We need a plan," said Kopaka.

"Yes. A plan," agreed Pohatu, looking hard at the Toa of Fire and Ice. "Not six plans, one for each of us."

"Very well," said Tahu. "We delay the creature as long as possible, while Turaga Vakama makes his escape. When we have fallen, Takua sees to it that this struggle occupies an honored place in the chronicles."

Lewa leaped up to a rocky ledge on the chamber wall. "I do not think I like this plan. Let's quickplot another."

But already it was too late for plans. With a roar so loud it almost knocked the Toa off their feet, the Rahi Nui emerged from the tunnel before the shocked eyes of Mata Nui's defenders.

It was bigger than anything any of them had ever seen, at least three times the size of a Toa. Its shape was right out of a Matoran's nightmare. The head of the beast was that of a Kane-Ra, the powerful Rahi bull, with long, sharp horns that could pierce solid rock with ease. Its forelegs were those of the Tarakava, the marine Rahi whose powerful arms could deliver a stunning blow to even a Takea shark.

Tahu instinctively cloaked the others in a shield as the creature padded into the chamber. Its body and hind legs were those of Muaka, the great cat whose powerful claws could shred solid protodermis. It also possessed the stinging scorpionlike tail of the Nui-Jaga, and a larger version of the Nui-Rama's insectoid wings.

"I never imagined my destiny would be to be flattened by a walking zoo," said Pohatu.

"Mata Nui is full of surprises," Gali replied. "This is not one of the pleasant ones."

The Rahi Nui looked from one Toa to another, as if trying to decide who posed the biggest threat. Strangely, its gaze lingered on Vakama, almost as if the beast remembered him somehow. Then Tahu moved between the Rahi and the Turaga of fire.

"Perhaps this creature is nothing but roar

and bellow," he said. "Let us see how he compares to the power of Hau Nuva."

The Rahi Nui stared at the little being who dared to stand in its path. Then it lowered its head and charged, striking Tahu's shield and sending the Toa of Fire flying across the chamber. Onua moved swiftly to put himself between Tahu and the stone wall, taking the impact on his own mighty body. Though neither was seriously hurt, both had the wind knocked out of them.

"Question answered," said Kopaka.

Lewa leaped from his perch, smiling. "I have a smartplan. Rahi still needs to airbreathe . . . so take away his air and down he falls."

Before anyone could react, Lewa had summoned the Mask of Speed and begun racing in tighter and tighter circles around the Rahi Nui. The Toa of Air could tell it was working, creating a vacuum around the beast. In another few moments, the Rahi would pass out from lack of air and the threat would be over.

The Rahi had other ideas. Its eyes tracked the green blur circling it for one pass, two, and then it lashed out with its foreleg. Lewa was moving too fast to stop when the long arm of a Tarakava suddenly appeared in his path. Tripping on it, he flew headlong into the chamber wall and slumped to the ground, stunned.

"We have barely begun, and already three of our number have fallen," said Gali. The Rahi Nui turned at the sound of her voice, its stinger slicing the air as it drew closer to the Toa of Water.

"You are still working as lone Toa," said Vakama. "The Rahi Nui is too powerful to be beaten that way."

"Then stop warning us and help," said Kopaka coldly. "If you know something about this beast, speak!"

Gali flipped through the air, narrowly avoiding the Rahi Nui's tail. The stinger struck the spot where she had been standing, shaking the chamber.

"It was bred for power, not intelligence," said Vakama. "That is how we were able to ... that it is how it was trapped here."

Lewa staggered to his feet, followed by

Tahu and Onua. Kopaka gestured for them to stay where they were, then turned to Pohatu. "Brother, we could use a bit of your speed . . . and your aim," he said, gesturing toward the ceiling.

"Gifts I gladly give!" answered Pohatu. The Toa of Stone shared the power of the Mask of Speed with his friends, endowing each with the ability to move at superspeed. "Let us give this beast's dull brain something to think about!"

The six Toa now circled the Rahi Nui. As soon as it would focus on one, that Toa would disappear in a burst of speed only to reappear somewhere else. Soon, all six were appearing in one spot for an instant, then vanishing again and popping up in another. The Rahi Nui reacted as if it were under attack by a swarm of gnats, snarling and swiping at empty air.

Pohatu saw his opportunity. He joined his climbing claws into a ball and flung it at the ceiling, shearing through a dozen stalactites. The sharp stones rained down on the Rahi Nui, further enraging the beast.

"I believe we have upset this creature."

Onua chuckled as he allowed the power of the Mask of Strength to fill his comrades. "Perhaps it can use some time off its feet."

Acting as one, the Toa slammed their fists on the floor. Their added strength created a massive shock wave that traveled to the center of the chamber, knocking the Rahi Nui onto its side. It bellowed and tried to right itself, but a second shock wave brought it down again.

"This is more joyfun than kolhii ball," said Lewa. "At least until we run out of ideas."

"Perhaps I can help," said Vakama. His voice filled the chamber, but there was no sign of him. The Turaga had invoked the power of the Mask of Concealment he wore. "Rahi! You have heard this voice before! It belongs to the one who trapped you so long ago!"

Tahu looked at Gali, both wearing expressions of surprise. Vakama, with his Noble Mask and his firestaff, had beaten this monster before? How was that possible?

The Rahi Nui rose again. It definitely did seem to recognize — and hate — that voice.

Worse, it could not see where the voice was coming from. It roared in rage.

"Do you remember the last time we met? Or are you too slow-witted?" taunted Vakama. "You howled and roared and even succeeded in harming some of my friends. But in the end, your rage was your undoing, monster."

The Rahi Nui was turning this way and that, trying in vain to find Vakama. Forgotten were the six Toa, who stood and watched as the beast grew more and more frenzied.

"Vakama does have a smartplan, doesn't he?" asked Lewa.

"Besides driving the beast wild? One can only hope," replied Onua.

"How long have you been down here, creature?" Vakama continued, still cloaked by invisibility. "How many suns have passed above? Did your master abandon you . . . or is he the reason we are here?"

Suddenly the shadows in the chamber grew darker still, and a cold wind chilled the Toa. A pair of massive, glowing red eyes appeared in the darkness of the tunnel and a harsh, grating voice said, "It has not been abandoned, Vakama. It has been waiting for your return."

"Makuta . . ." Gali whispered.

"But this beast wears no infected Kanohi Mask," said Tahu. "How does Makuta control it?"

"There is no need for a mask, Toa Tahu," said the voice of Makuta. "It hates Toa and all who stand with them. That is enough."

"And you skulk in the shadows, as you always have," Vakama snapped. "Striking through pawns because you are afraid to face the light."

Makuta laughed, a truly horrible sound. "Light? There is no light on Mata Nui. There never shall be."

"You have been defeated before!" shouted Vakama. "You shall be again!"

"Defeated? Never," hissed Makuta. "Only delayed. You cannot stop the darkness from falling, Vakama. No one can."

"We can, and we shall!" Tahu said, stepping forward, magma swords raised.

"Then do so," Makuta replied. "Defeat my Rahi, and you may leave this chamber. Fail, and Mata Nui is mine!"

The next instant, the eyes were gone, the chill had left the air, and the shadows were merely shadows once more. Makuta had left the Toa to their fate, sure that his victory would be won.

After a long moment, the Toa heard Vakama say, "Go."

Tahu, dodging a strike by the Rahi Nui, said, "What was that?"

"The beast can be distracted. Run for the tunnel."

"Toa do not run!" answered Tahu.

"Well, actually . . ." Onua muttered.

"They do when their Turaga tells them to do so!" Vakama's voice struck the Toa like a hammer blow. "Now go!"

The Rahi Nui snarled and started toward Vakama's voice. Gali grabbed Tahu's arm. "Only as far as the tunnel mouth, Tahu," she said. "We will not abandon Vakama."

"Would you make us cowards?" Tahu demanded.

"We don't have time to debate!" said Onua. "Come, fire brother, let us see what your Turaga has in mind."

Vakama waited until the Toa had slipped past the angry Rahi into the tunnel. Then he stood with his back to the chamber wall and willed himself to become visible again. He could hear Gali gasp and Tahu shout a warning, but he ignored them. His entire being was focused on the monstrous Rahi that confronted him.

"Come then, monster," he said. "Let us see what time has done to your power."

The Rahi Nui lowered its massive head, its claws pawing the ground. Its eyes locked on to Vakama's as it prepared to charge. Onua and Pohatu held Tahu's arms, keeping the Toa of Fire from racing into the chamber. "Trust him," Onua urged. "Vakama must know what he is doing."

The Turaga was not so certain. True, he had seen the Rahi Nui defeated once before. But that had been a long, long time past, and Vakama had been very different then. Perhaps it was his power that time had swept away, and not the Rahi's.

But now the time for questioning was over. The Rahi Nui charged, horns lowered and aimed right at Vakama. The Turaga counted the beast's huge strides and waited until he could feel the Rahi's foul breath on him. Then he leaped aside, turning invisible as he did, and listening for the satisfying crunch of Kane-Ra horns piercing stone.

He didn't have to wait long. The Rahi Nui slammed headfirst into the wall, burying its horns in the rock. Its charge had been so powerful that, once in, the horns couldn't be withdrawn. Try as it might, the Rahi Nui was stuck fast in the wall.

Cautiously, Vakama stepped away from the struggling creature and became visible once more. The six Toa stepped into the chamber and stood by his side.

"Will it ever get free?" asked Gali.

"In time, yes," said Vakama. "It will bring down the wall, if it must."

"I would rather not be here to see that," said Onua. "We have all our Kanohi Nuva Masks. The time has come to return to the surface."

"You took a great risk, Turaga," said Tahu as they walked into the tunnel. "If you had failed . . ."

"Then someone else would have stepped into my place as Turaga," answered Vakama. "Just as, someday, someone else may become Toa of Fire when your destiny has been fulfilled, Tahu."

"You knew what the beast would do."

"I hoped," said Vakama. "But I had to get it so angry it would forget how it had been trapped before. Whenua would say it was defeated because it forgot the past . . . Nuju, that it did not think about the future."

The Toa reached a dead end. Above them they could see the sky through an opening in the ceiling. "Now can we fly?" asked Gali, smiling.

The Mask of Levitation and the Mask of Speed combined to lift the Toa and Turaga aloft and carry them through the hole back onto the surface of Mata Nui. The Toa's quest for the masks was at its end, but their true ordeal still lay before them. For now, questions about their future as a team, the secrets of the Turaga, and what destiny held in store for Mata Nui had to be put aside. Somewhere the Bohrok-Kal were waiting, and six Toa, still lacking their elemental powers, had to find a way to defeat them.

Far below, deep in the darkness, Makuta laughed. "Ah, Vakama, Turaga of smoke," he rumbled. "Your secrets will be the end of the Toa yet."

When Vakama had finished his tale, Nokama walked up to him and laid a hand on his arm. "Now I understand, old friend, why you called this council."

"I never thought I would face the Rahi Nui again," answered Vakama. "Had I told the Toa about that beast long ago, perhaps they would not have been in such danger."

The other Turaga were silent. Even Onewa had nothing to say.

"We have told our tales," continued the

Turaga of fire. "And we have learned from them. The time has come to share all with the Toa. Are we agreed?"

The other Turaga nodded.

"Very well," said Vakama as the others rose. "I propose that we speak with them after the kolhii ball tournament. Surely nothing will happen there that will distract us from our purpose. . . ."

"We had best be going to the field, then, Vakama," said Nokama. "I am sure the Toa will have the wisdom and courage to understand all that we have to say."

With brief farewells to one another, the Turaga ended the council. They walked in silence to Ta-Koro, passing only Jaller on the way. The Captain of the Guard explained that his kolhii partner, Takua, had wandered off again and he was searching for him.

"Then search on, Jaller," said Vakama. "I am sure Takua has simply been distracted by some trivial matter. After all, what could be more important than the kolhii ball tournament?"

"Nothing!" Jaller shouted as he dashed away.

BIONICLE™

FIND THE POWER, LIVE THE LEGEND

The legend comes alive in these exciting BIONICLE™ books:

BIONICLE™ **CHRONICLES**

#1 Tale of the Toa
#2 Beware the Bohrok
#3 Makuta's Revenge
#4 Tales of the Masks

The Official Guide to BIONICLE™

BIONICLE™ Collector's Sticker Book

BIONICLE™: Mask of Light

BIONICLE

www.bionicle.com/thegame

THE GAME

Live the legend! Challenge the might of the Rahkshi in the exciting new BIONICLE video game!

FALL 2003

PLAY AS YOUR HEROES

USE YOUR AWESOME ELEMENTAL POWERS

BATTLE WITH YOUR ENEMIES

SIX MASSIVE ENVIRONMENTS

LEGO

ELECTRONIC ARTS™

Available on:
Nintendo GameCube™
PC-CD
PlayStation®2

EVERYONE
E
Fantasy Violence
CONTENT RATED BY